Orphaseena

WRITTEN BY SARA CURREY
ILLUSTRATED BY KAREN BERGHORST

I want to express my gratitude…

To the book designer extraordinaire, Julie Chen,
who took this dream and transformed it into a reality.

To a breath-taking illustrator and partner in crime, Karen Berghorst.
Each painting is a masterpiece.

To the editor-in-chief, Justing Holding,
whose keen, Aussie eye brought sense to my mess.

To my Barnabas. Your gift of encouragement gave me the courage
to go further, higher than I believed possible.

To my family and friends for cheering me on, running alongside
and praying me through this Orphaleena journey.

To my Savoir and King, Your relentless love sought me
and brought me back home…and it still does.

Copyright © 2017 Sara Currey. All rights reserved.
Illustrations © 2017 Karen Berghorst. All rights reserved.
Designed by Julie Chen
Published by Belong to Me Books, find us at www.belongtomebooks.com
Printed in PRC

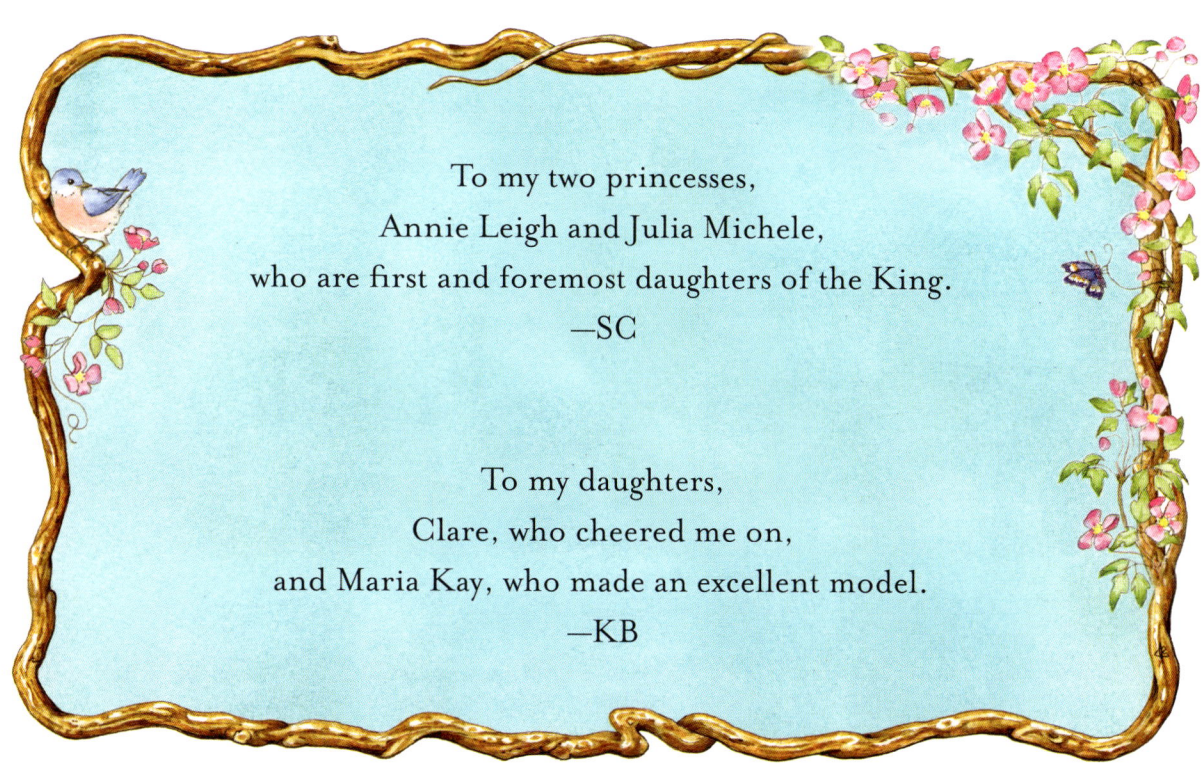

To my two princesses,
Annie Leigh and Julia Michele,
who are first and foremost daughters of the King.
—SC

To my daughters,
Clare, who cheered me on,
and Maria Kay, who made an excellent model.
—KB

There once was a girl named Orphaleena. For as long as she could remember, she had lived in the dungeon of a castle ruled by a terrible king. Her only friend and fellow prisoner, the Magician, had told her everything about who she was—how she had arrived as a child and how unfairly the King had treated her by condemning her to live in the prison.

Apart from the Magician, Orphaleena was alone in the dungeon. However, every now and then she would have a visit from the Man-servant. He was a kind man and she felt pity for him because he was always at everyone's beck and call. He was constantly attending to the needs of the King. Cleaning the castle, cooking the meals, dressing and tutoring the King's children were just a few of his duties. Yet, he never complained. It was as if he loved his work and Orphaleena loved every visit that she had from him. Just the sight of him brightened her darkest days.

Orphaleena spent many hours daydreaming about being a princess, a daughter and an heir of a good, kind king. Why was she an orphan? Who were her parents and what happened to them? Why had she been sentenced to live in a horrible dungeon under the rule of a tyrannical king?

Her unanswered questions would torture her until she could stand it no longer, driving her once again to ask the Magician to tell her the story of how she had arrived at the castle. He had time for her, unlike the King. He had all the time in the world, stuck down in that damp pit.

However, the Magician's answers made Orphaleena sad, even frightened. He recounted horrible, unimaginable stories of the King's rule and how her parents had abandoned her to this miserable place. She always ended up regretting having asked the Magician for answers.

One day the Manservant brought Orphaleena an invitation from the King himself. It was an invitation to a ball. Orphaleena wondered why the King would bother inviting her—a poor, dirty, unloved girl—to a fancy party. She was suspicious of his intentions and yet hopeful because he seemed to be taking an interest in her.

The first thing Orphaleena did was to share her puzzling news with the Magician. Trying to contain her building excitement and not look too eager, she explained her invitation to escape the walls of the dungeon for an evening of dancing till dawn. However, the sweet sliver of hope soon turned and pierced her heart as she listened to the painful truth. The only reason the cruel King would invite a prisoner to a ball, the Magician explained, was not to be a guest but to be the entertainment. She would be the clown, the jester, ridiculed in front of everyone!

Reluctantly and angrily, Orphaleena agreed. The Magician's words made sense. The King didn't request her presence at the ball because he cared about her; instead it was to put her on display. The only one who had ever cared for her was the Magician and now he was trying to protect her from getting hurt. Exhausted from the drama, she asked the Magician for some of his familiar potion to help her sleep and help her forget that she had ever been asked to the ball. He willingly gave it to her and the last thing she remembered was wishing she could see the kind Manservant. If she could just catch a glimpse of his gentle face, she would feel better.

It was the next afternoon when a loud crashing sound woke Orphaleena from her stupor. There was an explosion and smoke filled the prison cell. As she blindly searched for the Magician, she tripped over something … It was someone's foot! Lying on the dirty floor, she felt someone gently lift her to her feet. Then she came face to face with the Manservant.

"You called for me and I am here," he said.

Orphaleena still had a headache from the potion she had taken the night before. She didn't remember ever calling for the Manservant.

"Do you want to go?" he asked, interrupting her thoughts.

"Go? Go where?" She had forgotten the invitation.

"Do you want to go to the ball and leave this prison forever?"

"Why do I need to leave? This is my home. It's where I belong."

"Trust me—you do not really belong here. It is time for you to make a decision. Do you want to stay here or do you want to go with me, where you really belong?" he asked as a smile appeared on his lips.

"I want to go with you!" Orphaleena blurted out. She was taken aback by her bold words but she wasn't sorry. There was something about the Manservant that had always made her feel safe, cared for and loved.

"Follow me!" he ordered. "We don't have much time. The Magician will awaken and then you will be in trouble."

Orphaleena immediately followed the Manservant through the rubble, even though she didn't understand what he was talking about. Why would she be in trouble? Why would the Magician want to hurt her? She had believed that he was her friend.

The Manservant led her out of the dungeon and through the dark tunnels under the castle. The smells of sewer and the sound of rats scurrying about made Orphaleena feel faint. She stumbled, but her guide never let go of her hand.

After what seemed like an eternity, Orphaleena found herself climbing up a long flight of stairs towards a door. Suddenly, the door opened and daylight flooded in. It was hard to see clearly with so much sunlight. Her eyes had never actually seen the sun … or had they? The blinding light and the sun's warmth stirred a distant memory. Once she stopped squinting, she found herself standing in the middle of a beautiful garden. There were colorful flowers, bubbling fountains and ornate statues. She couldn't stop staring at the beauty of it all.

There, directly in front of her, was a towering structure … the castle! Hatred suddenly filled her heart for that place and its terrible king. Orphaleena recited to the Manservant all of the stories she had heard down in the dungeon.

"How can you work for that tyrant?" she demanded. "After all he's done, how can you serve him and his family? You are so humble and kind; it just doesn't make sense."

"Oh, Leena," the Manservant whispered, "you have been under the Magician's spell for so long that you don't even remember."

"Remember what?" she cried.

"You aren't an orphan. You are a daughter … a daughter of the King," he replied.

"Don't ever say such a horrible thing again!" she screamed. "Did you bring me here to betray me to him? Did he put you up to this? Take me back now! Take me back to my prison! I want to go back to the Magician. I need my potion. I'm not well!" And with that, Orphaleena collapsed.

When she awoke, Orphaleena was in the Manservant's arms. He was singing softly over her and she no longer wanted to escape his embrace, but to remain there for the rest of her life. He was singing a song and it was for her; it was her story. As she listened, questions she had asked were being answered and the constant fears she had battled were disappearing.

Did he just say that he loved her? Did he just say that the King was a good king? That her friend the Magician was an evil, spell-binding fraud? Orphaleena was shaken. Suddenly she felt as though she was waking from a dream that was too good to be true.

"Stop!" she screamed as she pushed herself free. "How can you tell me these lies? I trusted you. I followed you away from my home. You say the Magician lied to me, but how do I know that you're not lying to me, too? Who am I supposed to trust?" she cried in anguish.

The Manservant answered by slowly pulling his shirt open to reveal his chest. There was a distinct mark in the shape of a heart.

"You have one, too," he whispered.

Orphaleena froze. Her mouth went dry. What was he talking about? What heart mark? If she had one, she would surely know.

"All of the King's children have this birthmark," he smiled.

"What? We are children of a tyrant?" she retorted.

"Yes, and no. Yes, we are his children, but no, he isn't a tyrant. He is good and kind and loving and just."

"I don't believe you," she cried. "If he was any of those things, he wouldn't have allowed me to be imprisoned, or abandoned like an orphan!" She was screaming now, and hot tears were streaming down her face. "He doesn't love me!"

"Oh, Leena, he hasn't done any of the horrible things you're accusing him of. Those are all lies told by the Magician. He has brainwashed you and you've been deceived. His only power over you comes from his lies. Once you believe the truth—that the King loves you—the Magician's power will be destroyed!"

Orphaleena was so confused. She collapsed to her knees, exhausted. Her whole life she had believed that the King was her enemy, the Magician was her friend and she was an unwanted orphan. What if the Manservant was telling the truth? What if she was wrong? What if she was a daughter of the King, a real princess?

NO! This was crazy. She was ordinary. Her place was back in the dungeon, in the dark, with her fears, with the Magician.

"Leena!" cried the Manservant. "You didn't check."

"Check what?" Orphaleena sighed.

"Check your heart. Go ahead—look for the King's mark."

Orphaleena had no desire to check. She could feel the familiar sadness and pain overtaking her body, like so many times before. It was as if she could feel the Magician's potion taking effect on her mind and body.

"Please check—we don't have time to waste!" the Manservant pleaded.

She didn't know why she obeyed his plea, but Orphaleena stood up from where she had been kneeling. She turned and slowly looked down. There was the familiar spade mark on her chest, a reminder of all her hard work, toil and the fatigue she always felt. If this was the King's mark, he was even crueler than she had previously thought.

"You have the same birthmark as I do, as all of the King's sons and daughters do. He gives each child a heart when they are born—a piece of his own heart so that they will never forget who they are."

A heart? Orphaleena knew she didn't have one of those, only a spade. And then it became clear to her. She was the one who was mistaken. She had been looking at her birthmark upside down! The way she saw the mark was the opposite of the way the King saw it.

As soon as the Manservant's words sunk in, she felt all her anger and sadness dissolve. Had she never been deserted? How was this so? Orphaleena no longer wanted to hurry back to her prison. Instead she wanted to stay; she wanted answers to her questions.

"If I have the King's heart, then am I his daughter? And am I a princess? Do I have brothers and sisters? Are we related?"
The questions came tumbling out of her mouth.

"Yes, yes, yes and yes!" the Manservant exclaimed. "That's what I have been trying to tell you. Your father, the King, sent me to you yesterday to invite you to the ball — your ball. He wants to welcome you back home and has planned a party in your favor. That is, if you want to come home. Every day he stands in this very place looking for you, waiting to see if you will return. It's all for you. Look—here he comes!"

As soon as Orphaleena caught a glance of the King running towards her, she crumpled to the ground in shame. The hope that she had begun to feel began to fade and despair threatened to overcome her. How could she look into his pure eyes after blaming him for all of her pain and believing such ugly lies about him? Once he saw her filthy, pathetic state, he would surely send her back to the darkness. Orphaleena was turning to crawl back to the dungeon when she felt a large, gentle hand touch her head.

"Oh, Leena, my daughter! Leena, you've come, you've come!" And with that, he scooped her up in his strong arms and swung her around. She felt weightless and clung tightly to his neck. She couldn't resist his embrace and she didn't want to. She couldn't remember ever being held before and now both the Manservant and the King had hugged her in the same day. It felt so good.

"Oh, Leena, how I've missed you."

"Are we too late, my Lord?" asked the Manservant.

"No, my Son, we are right on time. Leena is the guest of honor."

As they walked towards the castle, hundreds of questions swarmed in Orphaleena's head like bees to a honeycomb. The most pressing of these was why the King kept calling her Leena and not by her real name, Orphaleena.

It was as if he read her mind.

"My dear Daughter," he said, "you have never been an orphan, just a lost child. You wandered away from the castle a long time ago but I have waited in hope of your return. As for the rest of your questions… we have an eternity for me to answer all of them."

And with that they entered Leena's welcome home ball.